The Rainbow Magic Collection

Volume 2: Books #5-7
plus an all-new bonus story!

Sky the Blue Fairy
Inky the Indigo Fairy
Heather the Violet Fairy
Hannah the Happily Ever After Fairy

by Daisy Meadows
illustrated by Georgie Ripper

SCHOLASTIC INC.

New York   Toronto   London   Auckland   Sydney
Mexico City   New Dehli   Hong Kong   Buenos Aires

ISBN-13: 978-0-545-06799-7
ISBN-10: 0-545-06799-5

Rainbow Magic #5: *Sky the Blue Fairy*, ISBN 0-439-74684-1,
Text copyright © 2003 by Rainbow Magic Limited.
Illustrations copyright © 2003 by Georgie Ripper.

Rainbow Magic #6: *Inky the Indigo Fairy*, ISBN 0-439-74685-X,
Text copyright © 2003 by Rainbow Magic Limited.
Illustrations copyright © 2003 by Georgie Ripper.

Rainbow Magic #7: *Heather the Violet Fairy*, ISBN 0-439-74686-8,
Text copyright © 2003 by Rainbow Magic Limited.
Illustrations copyright © 2003 by Georgie Ripper.

Rainbow Magic: *Hannah the Happily Ever After Fairy*,
copyright © 2006 by Rainbow Magic Limited.
Previously published as *Hannah the Happy Ever After Fairy*
by Orchard U.K. in 2006.

12 11 10 9 8 7 6 5 4 3 2 1   8 9 10 11 12/0

Printed in the U.S.A.   40

First Scholastic Printing, October 2008

Contents

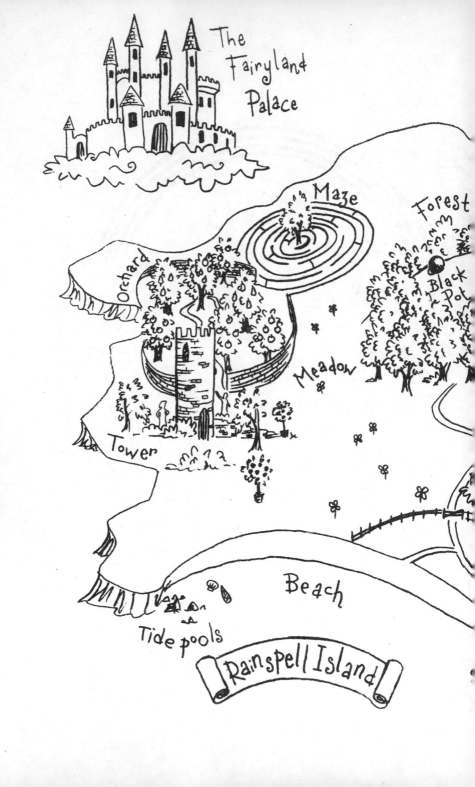

Cold winds blow and thick ice forms,
I conjure up this fairy storm.
To seven corners of the human world
the Rainbow Fairies will be hurled!

I curse every part of Fairyland,
with a frosty wave of my icy hand.
For now and always, from this day,
Fairyland will be cold and gray!

Sky
the Blue
Fairy

Sky
the Blue
Fairy

For everyone who
believes in fairies

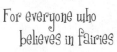

Special thanks to
Sue Bentley

A Magic Messenger

"The water's really warm!" Rachel Walker said, laughing. She was sitting on a rock, dipping her toes in one of Rainspell Island's deep blue tide pools. Her friend Kirsty Tate was looking for shells on the rocks nearby.

"Be careful not to slip, Kirsty!" called

☆⚝·☆·☆·☆⚝·☆

Mrs. Tate. She was sitting farther down the beach with Rachel's mom.

"OK, Mom!" Kirsty yelled back. She looked down at her bare feet, and a patch of green seaweed beneath them began to move. There was something blue and shiny tangled up in the seaweed. "Rachel! Come over here," she shouted.

Rachel hopped across the rocks. "What is it?" she asked.

Kirsty pointed to the seaweed. "There's something blue under there," she said. "I wonder if it could it be . . ."

"Sky the Blue Fairy?" Rachel said eagerly.

A few days before, Rachel and Kirsty had discovered a magical secret. The wicked Jack Frost had banished the seven Rainbow Fairies from Fairyland with a magic spell. Now the fairies were hidden all over Rainspell Island. Until they were all found there would be no color in Fairyland. Rachel and Kirsty had promised the Fairy King and Queen that they would help find the fairies.

The seaweed twitched.

Rachel felt her heart beat faster.

"Maybe the fairy is all tangled up," she whispered. "Like Fern was when she landed in the ivy on the tower."

Fern was the Green Rainbow Fairy. Rachel and Kirsty had already found Fern and her sisters Ruby, Amber, and Sunny.

Suddenly, a crab crawled out from under the seaweed at Kirsty's feet. The crab was bright blue and very shiny. Tiny rainbows sparkled across its shell. It didn't look like any of the other crabs on the beach.

Kirsty and Rachel smiled at each other. This must be more of Rainspell Island's special magic!

"Oh, no! Fairy in trouble!" the crab

muttered in a tiny voice. It sounded scratchy, like two pebbles rubbing together.

"Did you hear that?" Rachel gasped.

The crab stopped and peered up at the girls with his little stalk eyes. Then he stood up on his back legs.

"What's he doing?" Kirsty asked in surprise.

The crab pointed one claw toward some rocks farther along the beach, under the cliffs. He rushed forward a few steps, then came back and looked up at Rachel and Kirsty again. "Over there," he said.

"I think he wants us to follow him," Rachel said.

"Yes! Yes!" said the little crab, clicking

his claws. He set off sideways across a large, flat rock.

Kirsty turned to Rachel. "Maybe he knows where Sky is!"

"I hope so," Rachel replied, her eyes shining.

The crab moved off the rocks and headed across a stretch of sand. Rachel and Kirsty followed him. It was a hot, sunny day. Seagulls flew over the beach on strong, white wings.

"Rachel, Kirsty, it's almost lunchtime!" called Mrs. Walker. "We're going back to Dolphin Cottage."

Kirsty looked at Rachel in dismay. "But we have to stay here and look for the Blue Fairy!" she whispered.

The little crab jumped up and down, kicking up tiny puffs of sand. "Follow me, follow me!" he said. The girls couldn't leave him now!

Rachel thought quickly. "Mom?" she called back. "Could we have a picnic here instead, please?"

Mrs. Walker smiled. "Why not? It's a beautiful day. And we should make the most of the last three days of our

vacation. I'll head back to the cottage
with Kirsty's mom and make some
sandwiches. You girls stay out of the
water until we get back, OK?"

Only three days, thought Kirsty, *and three
more Rainbow Fairies to find: Sky, Inky, and
Heather!*

The two girls waved as their moms
headed off toward the cottages. Kirsty
turned to Rachel. "We'd better hurry.
They'll be back soon."

The crab set off again, this time over a
big slippery rock. Rachel and Kirsty

climbed
carefully after
him. Rachel
saw him stop next
to a small tide pool.
There were lots of pretty
pink shells in it.

"Is the fairy in one of the tide pools?" she asked. "Is it this one?"

The crab looked into the pool. He scratched the top of his head with one claw, looking puzzled. Then he hurried away.

"I guess not," Kirsty said.

"What about here?" Rachel said, stopping by another pool. This one had tiny silver fish swimming in it.

But the crab shook his claw at them and kept going.

"Not this one, either," said Kirsty.

Suddenly, Rachel spotted a large tide pool. It was all by itself, right at the foot

of the cliff. "Let's try that one," she said, pointing.

Kirsty ran over.

The sky was reflected in the surface of the pool like a shiny, blue mirror.

Rachel caught up with her friend. She leaned over and looked into the water.

The crab scuttled up behind them, his stalk eyes wiggling like crazy. When he dipped his claw into the pool, the water fizzed like ginger ale.

"Fairy!" cried the little crab, lifting his claw out of the water. Blue sparkles dripped off it and landed in the pool with a sizzle. The entire pool was shimmering with magic!

Bubble Trouble

"Thank you, little crab," Rachel said. She crouched down and stroked the top of the crab's shell.

The crab waved one claw at her, then dived into the water. He sank to the sandy bottom and disappeared under some seaweed.

Kirsty peered into the tide pool. "Can

you see the Blue Fairy, Rachel?" she asked.

Rachel shook her head.

Kirsty sighed, disappointed. "I can't, either."

"Do you think Jack Frost's goblins found her first?" Rachel said.

"I hope not!" Kirsty shuddered. "Those goblins will do anything to stop the Rainbow Fairies from getting back to Fairyland."

Just then, Rachel and Kirsty heard a sweet voice singing a song. "With silver bells and cockle shells, and pretty maids all in a row . . ."

"Oh!" Rachel gasped. "It's so pretty! Do you think it's the little crab?"

Kirsty shook her head. "His voice was all gritty."

"You're right," Rachel agreed. "This voice sounds tinkly — more like a fairy!"

"I think the singing is coming from that seaweed," said Kirsty, pointing into the tide pool.

Rachel peered into the water. She could see something unusual in the rippling seaweed. "Look!" she said.

Just then, a huge bubble came bobbing out of the seaweed. It floated toward the surface of the pool.

Rachel and Kirsty watched with wide eyes. There was a tiny girl inside the bubble! She waved at them and fluttered her rainbow-colored wings.

☆⁂☆ ☆ ☆⁂☆

"Oh!" Kirsty gasped. "It's her! I think we've found Sky the Blue Fairy!"

The fairy pressed her hands against the curved sides of the bubble. She wore a short, sparkly dress and knee-high boots the color of bluebells. Her earrings and headband were made of little stars.

"Please help me!" Sky said. Her tiny voice sounded like bubbles popping.

Suddenly, a cold breeze swept through Rachel's hair. A dark shadow fell across the tide pool. The glowing blue water turned gray. It was as if a cloud had covered the sun.

Rachel looked up. The sun was still shining brightly overhead. "What's happening?" she cried.

Kirsty heard a strange hissing sound. She glanced around in alarm.

A layer of frost was creeping across the rocks toward them, covering the beach in a crisp, white blanket.

"Jack Frost's goblins must be very close," Kirsty said, feeling worried.

Inside her bubble, Sky shivered as ice began to cover the tide pool.

"Oh, no! She's going to be trapped," Kirsty cried.

Sky's bubble had stopped bobbing in the water. Now it hung very still, frozen into the ice. Rachel and Kirsty could see that Sky looked very scared.

"Poor Sky! We have to rescue her!" Rachel exclaimed. "But how can we melt all that ice?"

"I know!" said Kirsty. "Why don't we look in our magic bags?"

The Fairy Queen had given Rachel and Kirsty bags with very special gifts in them, to use for helping fairies in trouble.

"Of course!" Rachel said. Then she frowned. "Oh, no! I left them in my backpack. It's on the other side of the tide pools, way down the beach!"

Goblins on Ice

"I'll run back and grab the magic bags," Rachel said, jumping quickly to her feet.

"OK," Kirsty said. She blew on her hands to warm them up. The frost was making the air very cold. "I'll stay here with Sky. But hurry!"

"I will," Rachel promised. She scrambled

☆⋆☆⋆☆⋆☆⋆☆

back over the rocks and onto the sandy
beach.

Rachel's backpack was lying right
where she'd left it. She reached inside and
pulled out one of the magic
bags. It was glowing
with a soft golden
light. When she
opened it, a cloud
of glitter sprayed
out. Rachel slid
her hand into the
bag. There was
something inside,
smooth like a
pebble. She pulled it
out and looked
closely at it. It was a tiny blue
stone, shaped like a raindrop.

Rachel was confused. The stone was pretty, but how could it help?

Just then, the blue stone began to glow in her hand. It became warmer and warmer until it was almost too hot to hold. As it grew hotter, it glowed fiery red. Rachel curled her fingers around the raindrop stone and smiled. They could use it to melt the ice and set Sky free!

She ran back to the tide pool as fast as she could. But when she reached the rocks, she stopped dead in her tracks. Kirsty was still standing by Sky's frozen pool, but she wasn't alone anymore. Two ugly goblins were skating on the ice next to her!

"Go away!" Kirsty was shouting at the goblins, waving her hands.

Rachel could tell that Kirsty was really angry. Rachel didn't feel scared, now that she had fairy magic to help fight the goblins.

"Go away yourself!" one of the goblins yelled rudely at Kirsty. He held his arms out to his sides and slid across the ice on one foot.

Kirsty tried to grab the other goblin,
but he dodged out of reach. "Can't
catch me!" he cried.

"Hee, hee! The fairy can't get out of the
bubble!" The other goblin laughed. His
bulging eyes gleamed as he did a little
twirl on the ice.

"We're going to get her out!" Kirsty
told him. "We're going to find *all* the

☆ ⭐ ☆ ☆ ⭐ ☆

Rainbow Fairies. And then Fairyland will get its colors back!"

"Oh no, it won't," said the goblin. He wrinkled his nose and stuck out his tongue.

"Jack Frost's magic is too strong," said the other goblin. "You girls can't do anything about it. Hey, look at me!" He pointed one foot behind himself and spun around the pool. But the ice was very slippery. He skidded sideways and crashed right into his friend.

Splat!

"Clumsy!" the other goblin snapped angrily.

"You should have moved out of the way," grumbled the clumsy one, rubbing his bottom.

Then the goblins tried to stand up. But their feet skidded in all directions and they fell over again in a heap. Rachel saw her chance. She ran to the edge of the pool and threw the magical blue stone onto the ice.

Suddenly, there was a *fizz* and a *bang*!
A shower of golden sparks shot into the
air and the ice began to melt. A big hole
appeared in the center of the pool.

"Ow! Hot! Hot!" yelled the goblins,
sliding around on the ice. They scrambled
to the edge of the pool and hurried
away, their big feet slapping on the rocks
as they ran.

"They're gone!" Kirsty said in relief.

Rachel peered into the pool. "I hope
Sky isn't hurt," she said.

All the ice had melted and the water
reflected the blue sky again. Sky's bubble
was floating just below the surface.

Rachel saw Sky sit up inside the bubble and look around. Her eyes were big and scared, and she looked very pale.

Kirsty put her hand in the water. It was still warm from the magic stone. "Don't be afraid, Sky," she said. Very gently, Kirsty moved her hand closer to Sky and poked her finger into the bubble.

Pop!

Sky tumbled out of the bubble and into the water. She swam up to the surface, her golden hair streaming behind her.

Kirsty leaned over and fished the fairy out. Sky felt like a tiny wet leaf. Kirsty

placed her gently on a rock in the sun.
"There you are, little fairy," she
whispered.

Sky propped herself up on one elbow.
Water dripped from every part of her, but
there were no blue sparkles now. "Thank
you for helping me," she
whispered in a weak
voice.

Kirsty frowned at Rachel. "Something's really wrong. All the fairies we found before had fairy dust. What happened to Sky's sparkles?"

"I don't know," said Rachel. "And she looks really pale, almost white."

It was true. Sky's dress was so pale that the girls could hardly tell it was blue at all.

Kirsty bit her lip. "It looks like Jack Frost's magic took away her color!"

Just then, the blue crab scuttled out of the

water and made his way across the rock
to Sky. "Oh dear, oh dear," he muttered.
"Poor little fairy."

Sky shivered and wrapped her arms
around her body. "I'm so cold and
sleepy," she whispered.

Kirsty felt a pang of alarm. "What's
wrong, Sky? Did the goblins get too close
to you?"

Sky nodded weakly. "Yes, and now I
can't get warm."

"We have to help her," Rachel said.

"But how?" asked Kirsty. She looked

down at Sky in dismay. The fairy was curled up in a tiny ball with her eyes closed.

Rachel felt tears sting behind her eyelids.

Poor Sky. She looked really sick. What was going to happen to her?

Little Crab's Great Idea

Rachel spotted something moving down on the rock. "Look!" she said. The little blue crab was wiggling his front claws wildly.

"He's trying to tell us something," said Kirsty.

The girls crouched down.

"Don't worry," the crab said in his gritty voice. "My friends will help us." He scurried up to the top of the highest rock and snapped his claws in the air.

"What's he doing?" Kirsty asked. Then she stared in amazement.

Lots and lots of crabs crawled out of the tide pools around them. Big ones, little ones, all different colors. Their claws made scratchy noises on the pebbles.

The blue crab wiggled his eyes and clicked his claws, pointing up at the sky, then down at the ground. His friends scrambled away in all directions. Their little stalk eyes waved around as they poked their claws into the cracks between the rocks.

Rachel and Kirsty looked at each other, confused. "What's going on?" asked Rachel.

All of a sudden, Kirsty spotted a tiny pink crab tugging and tugging at something in the rock.

With a crunch, the crab tumbled over backward. It held a fluffy white seagull feather in its claws. The crab scrambled up again, waving the feather in the air. One by one, the other crabs searched for more feathers. Then the blue crab waved them over to to the rock where Sky lay. Very carefully, he tucked the feathers around the Blue Fairy. His friends gathered more and more feathers, until the fairy was lying in a cozy feather bed.

"They're trying to warm up Sky with seagull feathers!" Kirsty said.

Rachel held her breath. There were so many feathers now that she couldn't see the fairy at all. *Will the blue crab's idea work?* she wondered.

There was the tiniest wriggle in the feather nest. A faint puff of blue sparkles fizzed up.

POP

41

It smelled like blueberries. One pale blue star wobbled upward and disappeared in the air with a *pop*.

"Fairy dust!" Rachel whispered.

"But there's not very much of it," Kirsty pointed out.

There was another wriggle from inside the nest. The feathers fell apart to reveal the Blue Fairy. Her dress was still very pale. She opened her big, blue eyes and sat up.

She looked up at Rachel and Kirsty. "Hello, I'm Sky the Blue Fairy. Who are you?" she said in a sleepy voice.

"I'm Kirsty," said Kirsty.

"And I'm Rachel," said Rachel.

"Thank you for frightening the goblins away," said Sky. "And thank you, little crab, for finding all these nice, warm feathers." She tried to unfold her wings, but they were too crumpled. "My poor wings," said the fairy, her eyes filling with tiny tears.

"The feathers have helped, but Sky still can't fly," Kirsty said.

"Maybe the other Rainbow Fairies can help," Rachel said.

Sky looked up excitedly. "Do you know where my sisters are?" she asked.

"Oh, yes," said Kirsty. "So far, we've found Ruby, Amber, Sunny, and Fern."

"They are safe in the pot at the end of the rainbow," Rachel added.

"Could you take me to them, please?" said Sky. "I'm sure they will help make me better." She tried to stand up, but her legs were too wobbly and she had to sit down again.

"Here, let me carry you," Rachel offered. She cupped her hands and scooped up the feather nest with the fairy inside.

Sky waved at the little blue crab and his friends. "Good-bye. Thank you again for helping me."

"Good-bye, good-bye!" The blue crab waved his

claw. His friends waved, too, their eyes shining proudly. They had never rescued a Rainbow Fairy before.

Kirsty and Rachel glanced at each other as they walked across the pebbles. Sky was being very brave, but the goblins had come closer to her than to any of the other Rainbow Fairies. And now the Blue Fairy was hardly blue at all!

Back to the Pot!

Rachel and Kirsty hurried across the
beach and into the woods. Rachel
carried Sky very carefully. The fairy lay
curled in a ball inside the warm feathers,
her cheek resting on her pale hands.

"Here's the clearing with the willow
tree," Kirsty said.

The smell of oranges hung in the air, tickling their noses. Rachel glanced around and spotted a tiny fairy. She was hovering over a patch of daisies, collecting nectar in an acorn cup.

"Look!" Rachel said. "It's Amber the Orange Fairy."

"Hello again, Rachel and Kirsty!" Amber fluttered over and settled on Rachel's shoulder.

Then Amber saw Sky lying curled up in Rachel's hand. "Sky! Oh, no! Sky, what happened? I have to call the others," she cried. She waved her wand and a fountain of sparkling orange bubbles sprayed into the air.

The other Rainbow Fairies fluttered up
all over the clearing. The air sparkled
with red, orange, yellow, and green fairy
dust. Bubbles, flowers, tiny butterflies, and
leaves sprinkled onto the grass.

Rachel and Kirsty watched as the
fairies gathered around Sky. The Blue
Fairy sat up slightly and gave a weak
smile, happy to see her sisters. Then she
flopped back into her nest of feathers.

☆ ☆ ☆ ☆ ☆ ☆ ☆

"Oh, Sky!" cried Fern, the gentle Green Fairy.

"Why is she so pale?" Sunny asked.

"The goblins got really close to her," Rachel explained. "They froze the pond. Sky was trapped in a bubble under the ice."

"Ooooh! That's terrible." Sunny shuddered.

"Kirsty shouted at them and tried to catch them," Sky whispered.

"Thank you. You are so brave!" said Ruby the Red Fairy, then she flew high into the air. "We must think of something to help Sky! Oh, I know! Let's ask Bertram for his advice!"

The fairy sisters sped toward the willow tree, their wings flashing brightly in the air. Rachel and Kirsty carried Sky over in her feathery nest.

The pot at the end of the rainbow lay on its side under the willow's hanging branches. The Rainbow Fairies were living there until all seven sisters had been found and they could go back to Fairyland.

As Rachel put Sky down next to the pot, a large green frog hopped out.

"Miss Sky!" he croaked, looking pleased.

"Hello, Bertram." Sky gave another weak smile.

"The goblins came very close to Sky, and now she's really cold. We have to make her warm so she gets her color back," Fern explained.

Bertram looked very worried. "Jack Frost's goblins are so cruel," he said. "You must all stay close to the pot so that I can protect you."

"Don't worry," said Sunny, giving Sky a hug. "You'll feel better soon."

Sky nodded, but she didn't answer. Her eyes started to close. She was so pale, her arms and legs seemed almost see-through.

Rachel and Kirsty watched the rest of the Rainbow Fairies exchange worried glances. "Oh, Bertram, what if the goblins have hurt Sky forever?" asked Fern. "What can we do to save her?"

The Fairy Ring

Bertram looked very serious. "I think it's time for you fairies to try a spell."

Amber frowned. "It might not work with only four of us. Rainbow Magic needs seven fairies!"

"But Bertram's right, we have to try," Ruby said. "Maybe we can do a *small* spell. Quick, let's make a fairy ring."

The Rainbow Fairies fluttered
into a circle in the air
above Sky.

Rachel noticed a
black-and-yellow
queen bee and a
small gray squirrel
watching from the
edge of the glade.
"Queenie and
Fluffy have come
to watch the spell,"
she whispered to
Kirsty. Queenie the
bee had helped Sunny
get her wand back after
the goblins stole it. Fluffy
the squirrel had carried
Fern, Rachel, and Kirsty back to

the pot when the goblins had
been chasing them.
"Ready, sisters!" said
Ruby. She lifted her
wand. *"In a fairy
ring we fly, to
bring blue color
back to Sky!"*
she chanted.
The other fairies
waved their wands.
Four different
colors of fairy dust
sparkled in the air —
red, orange, yellow, and
green. The dust covered
Sky in a glittering cloud as
she lay in the nest of feathers on
the soft green grass.

✫✫✫✫✫✫✫

"Something's happening!" Kirsty said.
Through the cloud of dust, she could see
that Sky's little dress and knee-high boots
were turning bluer and bluer. "The spell is
working!"

Whoosh!

A shimmering cloud of blue stars shot
into the air. They drifted up to the sky,
where they faded away with tiny *pop*s.

"We did it!" cheered Amber, turning a cartwheel in the air, while Sunny clapped her hands in delight.

"Hooray for Rainbow Magic!" shouted Ruby.

Sky yawned and sat up. She brushed the feathers away and looked down at herself. Her face lit up. Her dress was blue again! "My wings feel strong enough to fly now," she said. She flapped them twice, then zoomed into the air. She did a twirl, and her wings flashed with rainbows. "Thank you, sisters!"

The Rainbow Fairies gathered around
Sky, hugging and kissing her. The air
around them bubbled with fairy dust —
red, orange, yellow, green, and blue. It was
almost a whole rainbow!

Rachel and Kirsty grinned.

Fern swooped down and scooped up an
armful of seagull feathers. "You won't
need these anymore!" She
laughed, tickling Sky with a
long, white one.

"But I think I might know what to
do with them!" said Sky. She flew
down to the edge of the pot and peeked
in. "It's so cozy!" she said, admiring the
tiny chairs and tables made of twigs and
the giant shell bed. Then Sky fluttered
over to the rest of the feathers and
gathered them up. "I thought we could
put these on our bed. They'll be very
warm and soft."

Her fairy sisters looked delighted. "Thanks, Sky. What a good idea!" said Ruby.

"Let's have a welcome-home feast," said Fern. "With wild strawberries and clover juice."

Amber did another cartwheel.

"Hooray! Rachel and Kirsty, you're invited, too!"

"Thank you, but we have to go." Rachel looked at her watch. "Our moms will be waiting at the beach with our picnic."

"Oh, that's right!" Kirsty remembered, jumping up. She felt a little disappointed that she wouldn't have a chance to taste some fairy food. But she also didn't want her mom to be worried. "Good-bye! We'll be back again soon!"

The fairies sat on the edge of the pot and waved to the girls. Queenie, Fluffy, and Bertram the Frog waved, too. "Good-bye! Good-bye!"

☆ ☆ ☆ ☆ ☆ ☆ ☆

Sky fluttered in the air next to Rachel
and Kirsty as they walked back across the
clearing. Tiny rainbows sparkled on her
wings. Her dress and boots glowed bright
blue, and a blueberry smell filled the air.

"Thank you so much, Rachel and
Kirsty," she said. "Now five Rainbow
Fairies are safe."

"We'll find Inky and Heather, too,"
Kirsty said. "I promise."

"Yes," Rachel agreed.

As they made their way back to the
beach, Rachel looked at Kirsty. "Do you
think we can find them in time? We only
have two days of vacation left. And the
goblins are getting much closer. They
almost caught Sky today!"

Kirsty squeezed her friend's hand and
smiled. "Don't worry. Nothing is going to
stop us from keeping our promise to the
Rainbow Fairies!"

Inky
the Indigo Fairy

Inky
the Indigo
Fairy

Special thanks to
Narinder Dhami

A Fairy-tale Beginning

"Rain, rain, go away," Rachel Walker said
with a sigh. "Come again another day!"

She and her friend Kirsty Tate stared
out of the attic window. Raindrops
splashed against the glass, and the sky
was full of purplish-black clouds.

"Isn't it a terrible day outside?" Kirsty
said. "But it's nice and cozy in here."

69

She looked around Rachel's small attic
bedroom. There was just enough room for
a brass bed with a patchwork quilt, a
comfy armchair, and an old bookshelf.

"But you know what the weather
on Rainspell Island is like," Rachel
pointed out. "It could be hot and sunny
very soon!"

Both girls had come to Rainspell Island
on vacation. The Walkers were staying in
Mermaid Cottage, while the Tates were
in Dolphin Cottage next door.

Kirsty frowned. "Yes, but what about Inky the Indigo Fairy?" she asked. "We have to find her today."

Rachel and Kirsty shared a wonderful secret. They were trying to find the seven Rainbow Fairies, who had been cast out of Fairyland by mean Jack Frost. Fairyland would be cold and gray until all seven fairies had been found again.

Rachel thought of Ruby, Amber, Sunny, Fern, and Sky, who were all safe now in the pot at the end of the rainbow. Only Inky the Indigo Fairy and Heather the Violet Fairy were left to find. But how could the girls look for them while they were stuck indoors?

"Remember what the Fairy Queen said?" Rachel reminded Kirsty.

Kirsty nodded. "She said the magic would come to us." Suddenly, she looked scared. "Maybe the rain is Jack Frost's magic. What if he's trying to stop us from finding Inky?"

"Oh, no!" Rachel said. "Let's hope the rain stops soon. But what should we do while we wait?"

Kirsty thought for a minute. Then she walked over to the bookshelf. It was filled with dusty old books that looked like

they hadn't been read in a long time. She pulled one out. It was so big that Kirsty had to use two hands to hold it. "*The Big Book of Fairy Tales*," Rachel read out loud, looking at the cover.

"If we can't find fairies today, at least we can read about them!" Kirsty grinned.

The two girls sat down on the bed and put the book on their knees. Kirsty was about to turn to the first page when Rachel gasped. "Kirsty, look at the cover! It's purple. A really deep purplish-blue."

"That's indigo," Kirsty whispered. "Oh, Rachel! Do you think Inky could be trapped inside?"

"Let's see," Rachel said. "Hurry up, Kirsty. Open the book!"

But Kirsty had spotted something else. "Rachel," she said. "It's *glowing*."

Rachel looked more closely. Kirsty was right! Some pages in the middle of the book were shining with a soft bluish-purple light.

Kirsty opened the book. The ink on the pages was glowing indigo, too. For a minute, Kirsty thought that Inky might fly right out of the pages, but there was no sign of her. On the first page of the book was a picture of a wooden soldier. Above the picture were the words: *The Nutcracker.*

"Oh!" Rachel said. "I know this story. I went to see the ballet at Christmas."

"What's it about?" Kirsty asked.

"Well, a girl named Clara gets a wooden nutcracker soldier for Christmas," Rachel explained. "He comes to life and takes her to the Land of Sweets." They looked in the book and saw a colored picture of a Christmas tree. A little girl was asleep next to it, holding a wooden soldier.

On the next page there was a picture of snowflakes whirling and swirling through a dark forest. "Aren't the pictures great?" Kirsty said. "The snow looks so real."

Rachel frowned. For just a minute, she thought the snowflakes were moving. Gently, she put out her hand and touched the page. It felt cold and wet!

"Kirsty," she whispered. "It *is* real!" She held out her hand. There were white snowflakes on her fingers.

Kirsty looked down at the book again,
her eyes wide. Just then, the
snowflakes started to
swirl from the book's
pages, right into the
bedroom. They moved
slowly at first, then
faster and faster. Soon
the snowstorm was so
thick, Rachel and Kirsty
couldn't see a thing. But
they could feel themselves
being swept up into the air by the
spinning cloud of snow.

Rachel yelled to Kirsty, "Why haven't
we hit the bedroom ceiling?"

Kirsty reached for Rachel's hand and
held on tight. "Because it's magic!" she
replied.

The Land of Sweets

Suddenly, the snowflakes stopped
swirling. Rachel and Kirsty found
themselves standing in a forest, with their
backpacks at their feet. Tall trees towered
around them and crisp white snow
covered the ground. The girls certainly
weren't in Rachel's bedroom anymore.

Then Rachel realized where they were.

"Kirsty, this is the forest that was in the picture," she said, grabbing her friend's arm. "We're *inside* the book!"

Kirsty looked frightened. "Do you think Jack Frost brought us here?" she asked. "Or his goblins?" Jack Frost's goblins were always trying to keep Rachel and Kirsty from finding the Rainbow Fairies.

"I don't know," Rachel replied. Then she frowned. There was something strange about this snow. She bent down and gently touched a snowdrift.

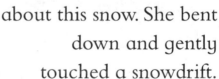

"This isn't snow." Rachel laughed. "It's powdered sugar!"

"What?" Kirsty looked amazed. She
scooped up a handful and tasted it.
The powdered sugar was cool and
sweet.

"Maybe this isn't Jack Frost's
magic after all," Rachel said.

"What's that?" Kirsty asked,
pointing.

Rachel could see a pink and
gold glow coming through the trees.
"Let's go find out," she said.

The girls picked up their backpacks

and headed toward the glow. It was hard
walking through the powdered sugar.
Soon their sneakers were covered in the
sugary snow.

Crack!

Rachel jumped as a loud noise echoed
through the trees.

"Sorry," said Kirsty. "I stepped on a stick."

"Wait," Rachel whispered. "I just heard
voices!"

"Do you think it could be goblins?"
Kirsty whispered back, looking scared
again.

Rachel listened. The voices were louder now. She sighed with relief. "No, they sound too sweet to be goblins' voices."

Rachel and Kirsty hurried toward the edge of the forest. When they came out of the trees, they saw that the glow was coming from a beautiful pink and gold archway.

"Look, Kirsty," Rachel gasped. "It's made of candy!"

Kirsty stared. The archway was made of pink marshmallows and golden caramel.

Then the girls heard the voices again, and they spun around. Two people dressed in fluffy, white coats were talking to each other and scooping powdered sugar into shiny metal buckets. They had round, rosy cheeks and small, pointy ears. They were so busy that they hadn't noticed Rachel or Kirsty yet.

"I think they're elves!" Kirsty whispered. "But they're the same size as we are. That means we must be fairy-sized again."

"We don't have any wings this time, though," Rachel whispered back.

Suddenly, one of the
elves spotted them. She
looked very surprised.
"Hello!" she called.
"Where did you
come from?"

"I'm Rachel and
this is Kirsty," Rachel
explained. "We came here through
the forest."

"Where are we?" Kirsty asked.

"This is the entrance to the Land of
Sweets," said the first elf. "My name is
Wafer, and this is my sister, Cone."

"We're the ice-cream makers," added
Cone. "What are you doing here?"

"We're looking for Inky the Indigo
Fairy," Kirsty told them. "Have you
seen her?"

Both elves shook their heads. "We've heard of the Rainbow Fairies," said Wafer. "But Fairyland is far away, across the Lemonade Ocean."

"Maybe you should ask the Sugarplum Fairy for help," Cone said. "She's so smart, she'll know what to do. She lives on the other side of the village."

"Could you take us to her?" Rachel asked eagerly.

The elves nodded. "Follow us," they

said together. Then they led Rachel and
Kirsty through the candy archway.

On the other side of the arch, the sun
shone down warmly from a bright blue
sky. Flowers made of whipped cream grew
underneath chocolate trees. Squishy pink
and white marshmallow houses lined the
street, which was paved with jelly beans.

"Isn't this great?" Kirsty laughed. "It's
like being inside a giant candy store!"

"And it all looks *yummy!*" Rachel
agreed.

 There were elves everywhere! Some had shiny buckets like the ice-cream makers, and others carried tiny, silver hammers. There were gingerbread men, too, looking very stylish in their bright bow ties and chocolate buttons. Then a whole line of tiny wooden soldiers in polished black boots marched across the street in front of them, and Rachel spotted a sparkling, pink, sugar mouse scurrying between their feet. Kirsty and Rachel smiled at each other. What a fun place this was!

The two elves led Rachel and Kirsty down the street. Suddenly, an angry-looking gingerbread man hurried out of one of the houses and bumped into Cone.

"Hello, Buttons," Wafer said. "Are you in a hurry?"

"What's the matter?" Cone asked. "You look upset."

The gingerbread man held out his hand. "Look at my best bow tie!" he said. "It was red when I hung it out to dry, and now it's *this* color!"

Rachel and Kirsty gasped. The bow tie
was purplish-blue!

"Inky!" they both said together.

The ice-cream elves looked confused.

"I think this means that Inky the
Indigo Fairy is close by," Rachel
explained.

"We'd better help you find her
before she causes any more
trouble," Cone said. Then
she frowned as a small
boy elf ran toward
them. He had one hand
over his mouth, and
he was laughing.

"Scoop!" called Wafer. She turned to
Rachel and Kirsty. "He's our little brother,"
she explained. "Scoop, what are you
giggling about?"

Still laughing, Scoop took his hand
away from his mouth. Rachel and
Kirsty stared. The little elf's mouth was
stained indigo!

"What happened?" Cone gasped.
"I had a drink from the lemonade
fountain," Scoop said between giggles.
"All the lemonade is a purplish-blue
color. It made my tongue tingle, too!"
"That sounds like more Rainbow Fairy
magic!" Kirsty said.

"Where's the lemonade fountain?"
Rachel asked the elves.

"In the village square," replied Cone.
"Just around the corner."

"Thanks for your help," said Kirsty.
She grabbed Rachel's hand and they
ran off.

As soon as Rachel and Kirsty turned
around the corner, they skidded to a halt.
In the middle of the village square was a
pretty fountain. Bright purplish-blue
liquid bubbled up from a fountain shaped
like a dolphin. A crowd of elves, soldiers,
and gingerbread men stood around the
fountain. They were all talking at once,
and they sounded angry! A polka-dotted
jack-in-the-box bounced back and forth
with a grumpy look on his face.

A swirl of indigo fairy dust shot up from the middle of the crowd. As the dust fell to the ground, it changed into blackberry-scented ink drops.

Rachel and Kirsty stared at each other. Fairy dust could only mean one thing. They had found another Rainbow Fairy!

Look Out!

"Inky!" Rachel called as she and Kirsty pushed their way through the crowd. "Is that you?"

"Who's that?" called a tiny voice.

Inky was standing by the edge of the lemonade fountain. She had neat blue-black hair and twinkling, dark blue eyes.

95

She was dressed in indigo jeans and a matching jacket that were covered with sparkly patches. Her wand was indigo, tipped with silver.

The fairy stared at Rachel and Kirsty with her hands on her hips. "Who are you?" she asked. "And how do you know my name?"

"I'm Kirsty, and this is Rachel," Kirsty explained. "We've come to take you back to your Rainbow sisters."

"We've found five of your sisters so far," Rachel added. "We're going to help you all go home to Fairyland."

"That's wonderful news!" Inky cried. "I've been so worried about them."

"How did you get to the Land of Sweets?" Kirsty asked.

"The wind blew me down the chimney of Mermaid Cottage, and into the *The Nutcracker* book," Inky replied. "I've been in the Land of Sweets ever since. But I can't go back to Fairyland and break Jack Frost's spell without my sisters. I have to get back to Rainspell Island first."

Before Rachel and Kirsty could say anything else, the crowd started shouting again.

"Look what she did to the lemonade fountain!" grumbled one elf.  Inky grinned at him. "I didn't mean to," she said. "The lemonade looked so yummy, I just had to take a drink. And that's when it turned indigo."

"And what about my bow tie?" snapped Buttons. He had followed Kirsty and Rachel to the fountain.

"I was really tired after walking through the forest," Inky explained. "I used your bow tie as a pillow while I took a little nap."

The crowd started to mutter angrily again.

Quickly, Rachel stepped forward. "Wait," she said. "Have you all heard about the Rainbow Fairies and Jack Frost's spell?"

The crowd listened as Rachel told them the whole story. When she'd finished, they didn't look angry anymore.

"I'm *so* sorry for all the trouble I've caused," Inky said. "Can you please tell us how to get back to Rainspell Island?"

"The Sugarplum Fairy can help you,"
said the jack-in-the-box, with a little
bounce. "Her home is just past the jelly
bean fields."

"That's where we were going,"
Kirsty said.

"Come on, then!" Inky cried. She
jumped forward and took Rachel and
Kirsty by the hand.

"Good luck!" everyone called.

Rachel and Kirsty walked along the
road toward the jelly bean fields while
Inky darted out eagerly ahead of them.
Just outside the village was a huge rock
made of hardened caramel. It was as tall
as a marshmallow house! Elves were
tapping the rock with little hammers to
break off pieces. Other elves picked up the
pieces and put them into silver buckets.

Kirsty nudged Rachel. "That looks like hard work," she said. "They don't seem to be collecting much caramel at all!"

Rachel peeked into one of the buckets as an elf walked past. Kirsty was right. There were only a few chips of caramel in it.

"Is there something wrong with the caramel?" Inky wondered.

The elf with the bucket overheard her.

"It's really hard today," he grumbled. "It almost seems like it has been *frozen*."

"Frozen!" Kirsty said in alarm. "Do you think that means Jack Frost's goblins are here, in the Land of Sweets?" The girls knew that whenever the goblins were close by, they brought frost and icy weather.

Inky looked scared. "I hope not,"
she said.

Just then, a loud, rumbling noise made
them all jump. "Look out!" someone
cried. An enormous wooden barrel was
rolling down the street, right toward
them! And running behind it were two
goblins with big, mean grins on their faces.

Stop Those Goblins!

"We've got you now, Inky!" shouted one of the goblins.

For a minute everyone froze. Then Inky leaped into action and gave Rachel and Kirsty a push. "Quick! Get out of the way!" she yelled.

The girls jumped aside just in time. The elves dropped their hammers and buckets.

They ran out of the way, too, bumping into one another in their panic.

Crash!

The barrel smashed right into the caramel mountain. Then it cracked open. Cocoa powder spilled out in a sticky brown cloud.

"Inky! Kirsty!" Rachel coughed, digging her way through the cocoa. "Are you OK?"

Rachel & Kirsty

"I think so!" Kirsty sneezed. *"Achoo!"*

"HELP!"

Kirsty heard Inky's frightened voice. But she couldn't see her through the cocoa cloud.

"Help!" Inky shouted again. "The goblins got me!" Her voice was getting fainter.

"Quick, Rachel!" Kirsty said. "Do you have our magic bags?"

Still coughing, Rachel swung her backpack around. Titania, the Fairy Queen, had given the girls bags full of magic gifts to help them rescue the missing Rainbow Fairies.

Rachel opened her backpack. Inside it, one of the magic bags was glowing. Rachel pulled out a folded paper fan from the bag. Puzzled, she opened the fan. It looked like the most beautiful

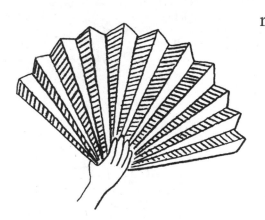

rainbow she had ever seen, with stripes of red, orange, yellow, green, blue, indigo, and violet.

Rachel thought for a minute. Then she began to flap the fan at the clouds of cocoa.

Whoosh!

A blast of air from the fan blew almost all of the cocoa away.

"Wow! This fan is amazing!" Rachel said as the last of the cocoa drifted off.

"Look, Rachel!" shouted Kirsty. "They're over there!"

The goblins had tied Inky's sneakers together with strawberry licorice. They were dragging her up the road, toward the jelly bean fields.

"We've got to save her," Rachel said, quickly folding the fan and putting it in her pocket. "Come on, Kirsty!"

"I'll go tell the Sugarplum Fairy," said one of the elves, and he ran off in the other direction.

Rachel and Kirsty ran up the road after Inky. The goblins had a head start, but Inky was wriggling and squirming so much that she was slowing them down.

The road led right through the jelly bean fields. Tall green plants stood in rows, each one covered with different-colored beans — pink, white, blue-spotted, and chocolate-brown ones. Elves were picking the jelly beans and putting them into big baskets.

Suddenly, Rachel noticed that the goblins were looking greedily at the jelly beans as they ran by with Inky. One of them skidded to a halt. He leaned over the fence and grabbed a big jelly bean from the nearest plant. The other goblin did the same.

"Yummy!" said the first goblin, stuffing the bean into his mouth.

"They're so greedy!" Rachel panted.

"Yes, but it gives me an idea of how to trick them!" Kirsty puffed. She started to run even faster.

The elves working in the field yelled at the goblins. But that didn't stop them. They gobbled down one bean after another. They picked beans with one hand and held on to Inky with the other.

"I have an idea," Rachel whispered to
Kirsty. On one side of the road she could
see some baskets full of jelly beans that
had already been picked. She hurried
over and grabbed a basket. Then she held
it out toward the goblins.

"Look what I have," she called. "A
whole basketful of beans!"

A Perfect Punishment

The goblins' eyes lit up
when they saw the basket. Inky
grinned and winked at Kirsty and
Rachel. She knew what they were
doing.

"Those jelly beans look yummy,"
Inky said to the goblins. "I wish I
could have one."

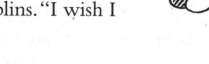

"Be quiet," snapped the goblin with the bigger nose. He turned to the other goblin. "You hang on to the fairy while I get the beans."

"No," said the other one. "You'll eat them all! You hold the fairy, and *I'll* get the beans."

"No!" roared the first goblin. "Then *you'll* eat all the beans!"

Glaring at each other, both goblins let go of Inky and ran toward Rachel.

She quickly threw an armful of beans on the ground and backed away. 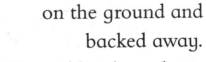 The goblins bent down to grab the beans. When they stood up again, Rachel threw another armful back down the hill, away from Inky.

Those greedy goblins just couldn't resist
the yummy jelly beans!

While the goblins were busy stuffing
themselves, Kirsty rushed over to untie
Inky. "Are you all right?" she asked.

Inky nodded and wriggled her feet free
from the licorice ropes. "Thank you!"

Rachel put the basket on the ground
and ran over to Kirsty and Inky. The
goblins pounced on the basket and began
arguing over the rest of the jelly beans.

"Let's get out of here before they realize that Inky is free!" Rachel said.

Suddenly, there was a gentle flapping noise overhead. Rachel looked up to see a huge butterfly with pink and gold wings fluttering above them. On its back sat a fairy with long, red hair.

The butterfly landed lightly on the ground. The fairy climbed off the butterfly's back and smiled at Inky and the girls. She wore a long green and gold dress and a tiara.

"Hello," she said. "I am the Sugarplum Fairy." She looked sternly at the goblins who were crouching beside the empty jelly bean basket. "What are *you* doing in the Land of Sweets?" she demanded.

The goblins didn't answer. They were too busy groaning and holding their stomachs.

"Oooh!" moaned the goblin with the big nose. "My tummy hurts."

"Mine, too," whined the other one. "I feel sick."

"They ate too many jelly beans!" Inky said, grinning at Rachel and Kirsty.

The Sugarplum Fairy looked even angrier. "You must be taught a lesson," she said to the goblins, "since you have stolen so many of our delicious jelly· beans."

"Why don't you make them pick more jelly beans?" Inky suggested.

"What a good idea." The Sugarplum Fairy smiled.

"That doesn't seem like a very bad punishment," Kirsty whispered to Rachel.

"But just look at the goblins' faces," Rachel whispered back.

The goblins looked horrified at the
thought of more jelly beans! They tried to
get up, like they wanted to run away. But
the Sugarplum Fairy waved her hand
and a few elves came running out of the
jelly bean fields. They marched the
goblins into the nearest field and handed
them empty baskets. With sulky faces, the
goblins started to pick the jelly beans.

"Serves them right!" Inky laughed.
Then she looked worried again. "But I still
need to get back to my Rainbow sisters."

"Please, can you help us get back to
Rainspell Island?" Rachel asked the
Sugarplum Fairy. "We would use fairy
magic to fly back, but we don't know
how to get there!"

The beautiful fairy nodded. "We will
send you home by balloon!"
she said. She waved her
wand at the empty jelly
bean basket. Rachel
and Kirsty watched in
amazement as it grew
bigger and bigger.
"But where's the
balloon?" asked
Rachel.

The Sugarplum
Fairy pointed to a
tall tree, covered with
pink blossoms.

"What pretty flowers,"
Kirsty said. Then she took
a closer look and began to laugh.
"They're not flowers. They're pieces of
bubble gum!"

"How is that going to help?" Rachel
was confused.

Inky grinned at them, her eyes
sparkling mischievously.
"Leave it to me!" she said.
She pulled one of the
bubble-gum flowers off
the tree, popped it
into her mouth, and
began to chew.

Then, squeezing her eyes shut tight, Inky blew a huge, purplish-blue bubble. She puffed and puffed, and the bubble grew bigger and bigger. Soon, it towered above them. It was the biggest bubble Rachel and Kirsty had ever seen!

Inky took the bubble out of her mouth and tied a knot in the end. "The perfect balloon!" she said. "Now, we're ready to go."

Rachel and Kirsty grinned at each other. What a wonderful way to travel back to Rainspell Island!

The elves helped tie the bubble-gum balloon to the basket. Then, Rachel, Kirsty, and Inky climbed inside.

The Sugarplum Fairy waved her wand at the balloon, showering it with gold sparkles.

"The balloon will take you back to Rainspell Island," she explained.

"Good-bye, and good luck."

"Thank you," called Rachel and Inky.

But Kirsty was looking around in dismay. "There's no wind!" she said. "We won't be able to get off the ground!"

The Bubble-gum Balloon

Rachel looked over at the leaves on the
bubble-gum tree. Kirsty was right. They
weren't moving at all!

The Sugarplum Fairy smiled. "Rachel,
don't you remember what you have in
your pocket?" she said.

"Of course!" Rachel exclaimed. "The
magic fan!" She took it out of her pocket

and unfolded it. Then, she flapped it
under the balloon.

Whoosh!

The blast of air lifted the balloon up
into the sky. "Good-bye!"
Kirsty called, waving at the
Sugarplum Fairy and all
the elves.

"Thank you for all
your help," Inky
said. "Sorry I made
such a mess!" she
added with a giggle.
The balloon bobbed
slowly upward. As it got
higher, the wind became
stronger, so Rachel put the fan back
in her pocket. Big, puffy clouds began
swirling around the balloon.

"We'll be home soon," Rachel said,
trying to sound cheerful.

The wind roared around them, rocking
the basket from side to side. Rachel, Kirsty,
and Inky hung on to one another and
squeezed their eyes shut.

Then, all of a sudden, the wind
dropped. The balloon stopped swaying.
The air felt warm.

Kirsty opened her eyes. "We're home!"
she gasped.

They were back in Rachel's attic
bedroom at Mermaid Cottage. The
balloon and the basket had vanished. The
book of fairy tales was lying on the floor,
open to *The Nutcracker*.

"But where's Inky?" Rachel said.

"I'm in here!" said a small, cheerful voice. The Indigo Fairy popped up from Rachel's pocket. She wriggled out and fluttered into the air, her wings sparkling with rainbows and showering the room with fairy dust ink drops. The smell of blackberries filled the air as they popped.

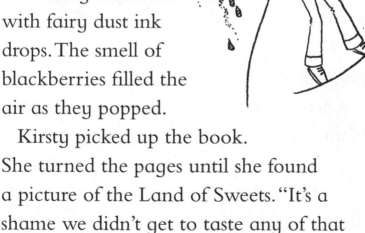

Kirsty picked up the book. She turned the pages until she found a picture of the Land of Sweets. "It's a shame we didn't get to taste any of that wonderful candy," she said.

As she spoke, a tiny puff of powdered sugar floated out of the book. Then, a shower of different-colored jelly beans fell onto Rachel's bed.

"They must be a present from the Sugarplum Fairy!" Inky laughed.

Rachel and Kirsty each popped a jelly bean into their mouth. They were tiny, but they tasted delicious!

"Yum!" said Inky, munching a bean. "Can we take some back to the pot for my sisters?"

Rachel nodded. "Let's go right away," she said, filling her pockets with jelly beans. "Your sisters will be waiting for you." She looked at Kirsty and smiled. They had escaped the goblins and rescued another fairy. They'd even been inside a fairy tale. And, now, there was only one more fairy to find! Rachel and Kirsty were so close to bringing the color back to Fairyland, they could almost taste it!

Heather
the Violet
Fairy

For everyone who has
felt fairy magic

Special thanks to
Sue Bentley

Message on a Kite

"I can't believe this is the last day of our vacation on Rainspell Island!" said Rachel Walker. She gazed up at her kite as it flew through the clear blue sky.

Kirsty Tate watched the purple kite soar above the field next to Mermaid Cottage. "But we still have to find Heather!" she reminded Rachel.

139

Jack Frost had cast a wicked spell that banished the seven Rainbow Fairies to Rainspell Island. And without the Rainbow Fairies, Fairyland had lost all of its color! The Fairy King and Queen had asked Kirsty and Rachel to help find the fairies. The girls had already found Ruby, Amber, Sunny, Fern, Sky, and Inky. Now they had only Heather the Violet Fairy left to find. Rachel felt a tug on the kite's string. She looked up. Something violet and silver flashed at the end of the kite's long tail. "Look up there!" she shouted. Kirsty shaded her eyes with her hand. "What is it? Do you think it's a fairy?" she asked.

"I'm not sure," Rachel said, pulling in the string.

As the kite came floating toward them, Kirsty saw that a long piece of violet-colored ribbon was tied to its tail. She helped Rachel untie the ribbon and smooth it out on the ground.

"It has tiny silver writing on it," Rachel said.

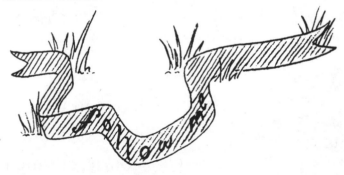

Kirsty crouched down to have a closer look. "It says, *follow me.*"

Suddenly, the ribbon was swept up by the breeze. It fluttered across the field.

"It must be leading us to Heather!" Kirsty said, jumping up.

Rachel gathered up her kite. "Mom, is it OK if we go exploring one last time?" she called.

Mrs. Walker was talking to Kirsty's mom in the yard outside Mermaid Cottage. Kirsty's family was staying in Dolphin Cottage, right next door. "Of course, as long as Kirsty's mom agrees," Mrs. Walker replied.

"It's fine by me," said Mrs. Tate. "But don't go too far. The ferry leaves at four o'clock."

"We'll have to hurry!" Rachel whispered to Kirsty.

The girls ran through the soft, green grass, following the ribbon. It bobbed and drifted on the breeze.

Suddenly, the ribbon flew out of sight behind a thick hedge.

"Where did it go?" Kirsty wondered.

"Through here!" Rachel said, pulling back one of the branches.

Kirsty followed her friend through the hedge. Luckily, the leaves weren't too prickly. On the other side, they found a path and a gate. There was a sign on the gate, in purple paint, that read: SUMMER FAIR TODAY!

Kirsty and Rachel walked through the
gate and into a pretty garden. There were
stalls full of cotton candy and ice cream
at the edge of a smooth, green lawn.
People roamed everywhere, chatting and
laughing.

"Isn't this great?" Rachel said, looking
around in surprise. A woman with a little
girl holding a bunch of balloons smiled
at her.

Suddenly, Kirsty spotted the ribbon fluttering toward a merry-go-round at the far end of the lawn. It wrapped itself around the golden flagpole and danced in the breeze like a tiny flag.

"It must be leading us to the merry-go-round!" Kirsty said. She grabbed her friend's hand and they ran across the grass together. The merry-go-round was as pretty as a fairy castle. Rachel stared at the circle of wooden horses on their shiny golden poles. They were beautiful!

"Hello there!" called a friendly voice behind them. "I'm Tom Goodfellow. Do you like my merry-go-round?"

Rachel and Kirsty turned to see an old man with white hair and a kind smile. "Yes, it's wonderful," Rachel said.

Kirsty watched the wooden horses rising and falling in time to the cheerful music. "Look, Rachel." She gasped. "The horses are all painted in rainbow colors! There's red, orange, yellow, green, blue, indigo, and violet."

Rachel looked more closely. Through the spinning horses, she could see that the pillar in the center of the merry-go-round was decorated with a picture of rainbow-colored horses galloping along a beach.

Just then, the merry-go-round slowed down and the music stopped. Mr. Goodfellow climbed up to help the riders off their horses. "All aboard for the next ride!" he called. Lots more excited children began to climb up onto the horses.

Mr. Goodfellow smiled down at Rachel and Kirsty. "How about you two?" he asked, his blue eyes twinkling.

A Magical Ride

"We'd love to take a ride on your merry-go-round!" said Kirsty. "Quick, Rachel, there are only two horses left!" She scrambled up onto one of them. A name was painted, in gold, on the saddle. "My horse is named Indigo Princess," Kirsty said, stroking the horse's shiny coat.

Rachel climbed onto a pretty horse next to Kirsty's. It had a lilac-colored coat and a silver mane. "Mine is named Prancing Violet."

"Hold on, everyone!" Mr. Goodfellow called out.

The music started and the merry-go-round began to turn. Prancing Violet and Indigo Princess swooped up and down on their painted poles.

Rachel laughed out loud as the

merry-go-round spun faster and faster.
The garden flashed by, and the
flowers and paths disappeared in
a blur. The sounds of music
and laughter faded away.
Rachel's heart skipped
a beat. Now, the only
horse she could see
was Kirsty's horse,
Indigo Princess.
Suddenly, she could
feel Prancing
Violet's hooves
thudding on the ground
beneath her.
Kirsty felt a sea breeze
whirling through her hair. Indigo
Princess seemed to toss her head and
kick up sand as she galloped along.

"Wow!" Kirsty exclaimed, tasting salt spray on her lips. "This is like riding a real horse!"

"It's awesome!" Rachel agreed. She felt as if they were racing along a beach, just like the horses she'd seen in the painting on the merry-go-round.

But before Rachel could say anything else, the horses began to slow down. The sandy beach faded away, and the sound of music returned. The merry-go-round came to a smooth stop.

Kirsty patted Indigo Princess's neck as she dismounted. "Thanks for the special ride!" she whispered. Then she turned to Rachel. "This merry-go-round is definitely magical, but where is Heather the Violet Fairy?"

Rachel slipped off of Prancing Violet's saddle and frowned. "I don't know," she said. Then she heard a tiny laugh coming from behind her. Rachel turned around. There was nobody there, just the picture on the pillar in the middle of the merry-go-round.

Rachel blinked. There was a fairy riding the violet-colored horse in the picture! She wore a short purple dress, high purple knee socks, and ballet slippers. A few purple flowers were tucked behind one of her ears.

"Kirsty!" Rachel whispered, pointing. "I think we found Heather the Violet Fairy!"

The Seventh Fairy

Mr. Goodfellow was still helping the other riders off the horses. Quickly, Rachel and Kirsty squeezed past the other horses to look more closely at the pillar.

"Heather must be trapped in the painting!" Rachel said.

"We have to get her out!" Kirsty said.

"Yes," Rachel agreed. "But what can we do with all these people around?"

Just then, almost as if he had heard them, Mr. Goodfellow clapped his hands. "Follow me, everyone. The clowns are here!"

A cheer went up as everyone ran across the lawn toward the clowns. Rachel and Kirsty were left alone.

"Now's our chance!" Kirsty said.

Rachel had an idea. "I know! Let's use our magic bags," she said. Titania, the Fairy Queen, had given Kirsty and Rachel bags of special gifts to help them rescue the Rainbow Fairies.

"Of course! I have mine here." Kirsty put her hand in her pocket and took out her magic bag. It was glowing with a soft, golden light. When she opened it, a cloud of glitter fizzed up into the air.

Kirsty slipped her hand into the bag. She felt something inside, long and skinny like a pencil. It was a tiny golden paintbrush.

Kirsty was confused. "What good is that? We don't want to paint any *more* pictures."

"Maybe Heather knows what we can use it for," Rachel suggested. "Amber told us how to help her when she was trapped in the shell, remember?"

"Good idea," Kirsty said. As she bent closer to the pillar, the tip of the brush touched the painted fairy's hand.

Suddenly, the whole picture glowed, and the fairy's tiny fingers moved!

A single violet-scented petal floated down from the picture. "Look!" Rachel gasped. "The brush is working some magic on the painting!" Kirsty whispered.

She began to stroke the brush all around the outline of the fairy.

At first, nothing seemed to happen. Then, the picture glowed even brighter. The fairy shivered. "That tickles!" she said with a tiny laugh.

The magic brush was lifting Heather out of the painting!

Rachel checked to make sure that no one was watching them. Then, with Kirsty's last stroke, the fairy sprang out of the painting, her wings flashing like jewels. Purple fairy dust shot everywhere, turning into violet-scented flowers that floated around her.

"Thank you so much for rescuing me!" said Heather, floating in front of them. She held a purple wand, tipped with silver. "I'm Heather the Violet Fairy! Who are you? Do you know where my Rainbow sisters are?"

"I'm Rachel, and this is Kirsty," said Rachel. "Your sisters are all safe in the pot at the end of the rainbow."

"Hooray!" Heather did a twirl of excitement, scattering violet sparks around the girls. "I can't wait to see them again." Kirsty held out her hand and Heather landed gently on it.

Kirsty hid her from view until the girls had run through the garden, past all the people watching the clowns. They ran out of the gate and down the path that led to the woods.

Deep inside the woods was a peaceful clearing with a willow tree on one side. The pot at the end of the rainbow was hidden under its long branches.

As soon as Rachel

and Kirsty reached the clearing, there was a shout from inside the pot. Inky the Indigo Fairy zoomed out. "Heather! You're safe!" she cried. "Look, everybody! Rachel and Kirsty have found our missing sister!"

The other Rainbow Fairies were close behind Inky. Sunny even flew out of the pot on the back of a huge bumblebee! The air flashed and fizzed with scented bubbles, flowers, leaves, stars, ink drops, and tiny butterflies. Bertram the frog

hopped out from behind the pot with a huge smile on his broad, green face.

As the fairies flew up to hug and kiss Heather, her blossom-filled fairy dust mingled with theirs, and the smell of violets filled the clearing.

"We *knew* you were coming," said Amber the Orange Fairy, doing a cartwheel in the air. "I've been feeling extra magical all morning!"

Rachel and Kirsty held hands and
danced in a circle. They'd done it! They
had found all seven Rainbow Fairies!

"And who is this?" Heather asked
Sunny the Yellow Fairy, reaching out to
tickle the queen bee under her chin.

buzzzzzz

"This is Queenie," said
Sunny, kissing the bee's
furry head. "She rescued
my wand after the
goblins stole it."

Ruby the Red Fairy's wings sparkled as she fluttered down and landed on Rachel's shoulder. "Thank you, Rachel and Kirsty," she said.

"You are true fairy friends," added Fern the Green Fairy, drifting onto Kirsty's hand. "And

now that we're all together again, we must use our magic to make a rainbow that will take us back to Fairyland." Suddenly, Rachel heard a strange

crackling sound. She spun around.
The pond at the edge of the clearing
wasn't blue anymore. It was white and
cloudy with ice! Rachel and Kirsty
and the fairies looked at one another
in alarm.

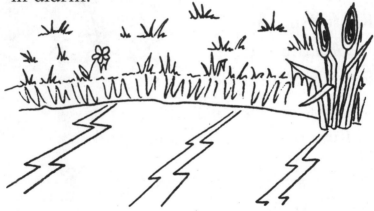

"Goblins!" they whispered. Sky the Blue
Fairy shivered with fright and fluttered
closer to Sunny and
Queenie for
protection.

Inky's tiny teeth chattered. "B-b-but it can't be. The Sugarplum Fairy kept them in the Land of Sweets, picking jelly beans!"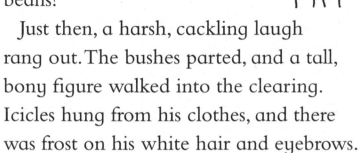

Just then, a harsh, cackling laugh rang out. The bushes parted, and a tall, bony figure walked into the clearing. Icicles hung from his clothes, and there was frost on his white hair and eyebrows.

It was Jack Frost!

Fairy Spells

"So, you are all together again!" Jack Frost cackled. His angry voice sounded like icicles snapping in half.

"Yes, thanks to Rachel and Kirsty," Ruby answered bravely. "And now we want to go home to Fairyland!"

Jack Frost gave a laugh like hailstones cracking against a window. "I will never

allow that!" he told them. But before Jack Frost could do anything, Ruby the Red Fairy flew high into the air.

"Come on, Rainbow Fairies! Now that we're together again, all of our Rainbow Magic has come back. This time, we must try to stop Jack Frost with a spell. Follow me!" she called.

Immediately, Inky shot to her sister's side, and turned to face Jack Frost with her hands on her hips and a determined look on her face. The other fairies flew to join them, and they all lifted their wands, chanting together:

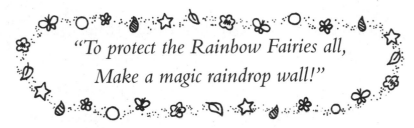

"To protect the Rainbow Fairies all,
Make a magic raindrop wall!"

Kirsty held Rachel's hand and watched, feeling very scared. Would the spell work?

A rainbow-colored spray shot out of each wand and a shining wall of raindrops appeared. It hung like a waterfall between the fairies and Jack Frost.

Rachel and Kirsty both held their breath.

"It will take more than a few raindrops to stop me!" Jack Frost hissed. He pointed one bony finger at the shimmering wall.

At once, the raindrops turned to ice. They dropped onto the frosty grass, like tiny glass beads, and shattered.

All the fairies looked horrified. Sunny
and Sky gave cries of dismay, and Inky
clenched her fists. Fern, Amber, and Ruby
hugged one another tightly. Heather
hovered off to one side, looking like she
was thinking hard.

Rachel and Kirsty stared in alarm as Jack Frost lifted his hand again.

Then Heather flew forward, waved her wand, and cried:

*"To stop Jack Frost
from causing trouble,
Catch him in a magic bubble!"*

A gleaming bubble popped out of the end of Heather's wand. It grew bigger and bigger. It looked like it was made of pale lilac glass. Jack Frost started to laugh, and stretched out his icy fingers. But before he could do anything else, there was a loud fizzing sound. Jack Frost disappeared!

Rachel blinked.

Heather's spell had trapped Jack Frost *inside* the bubble! It bobbed gently down onto the grass. Jack Frost pressed his hands against the shiny wall and looked furious.

"Great job, Heather!" Fern exclaimed.

"Quick, everyone. We must get into the pot and make a rainbow to take us back to Fairyland!" Heather urged. "Jack Frost could still escape!"

Rachel and Kirsty held the branches of the willow tree out of the way so that the fairies could fly through.

Heather's tiny eyebrows shot up as a squirrel scampered down the willow tree's trunk, toward the pot. "Who are you?" she asked.

"This is Fluffy," said Fern, stroking the squirrel. "He helped me escape from the goblins."

"Fluffy and Queenie will have to go back to their homes now," said Sky sadly.

"Can't they live with you in Fairyland?" Rachel asked.

"No, their homes are here, on Rainspell Island," Fern explained. "But we'll come and visit them, won't we?" All the fairies nodded, and Sunny wiped away a tiny tear.

Fern reached up to give Fluffy one last hug. Her sisters fluttered around, saying good-bye to Queenie and Fluffy.

"Thank you again for all your help," said Ruby.

Queenie buzzed good-bye as she flew away. Fluffy gave a farewell flick of his tail, then scampered off.

Heather fluttered in front of Rachel
and Kirsty. "Would you like to come
to Fairyland with us? I'm sure Queen
Titania and King Oberon will want to
thank you."

Rachel and Kirsty nodded eagerly.
Heather smiled and waved her wand,
sprinkling the girls with
purple fairy dust.

Kirsty felt herself
shrinking. The grass
seemed to rush toward
her. "Hooray! I'm
a fairy again!"
she cried.

Rachel
laughed as wings
sprang from her
shoulders.

Just then, there was a yell from inside
the giant bubble.

Rachel and Kirsty looked around.

Jack Frost was looking very scared. His
face was bright red, and drops of water
ran down his cheeks. He was *melting*!

"Well, he can't stop
you from getting to
Fairyland now,"
said Kirsty.

But Sky's tiny
wings drooped. She
hovered in the air,
looking sad. "Without
Jack Frost, there will
be no seasons," she
pointed out. "We
need his cold and
ice to make winter."

"No winter?" Inky said, looking shocked. "But I love sledding in the snow and skating on the frozen river."

"Without winter, when will we have spring?" Amber said in a small voice. "What will happen to all of the beautiful spring flowers?"

"And the bees need the flowers to make honey in summer," Sunny said sadly.

"After summer, autumn comes. That's when the squirrels find nuts to store for hibernation," said Fern.

"We need all the seasons, you see," said Sky. "If we leave Jack Frost in that bubble . . ."

The fairies looked upset. Then, Heather spoke up. "This is all true. But I also feel sorry for Jack Frost. He looks very frightened."

"Heather's right. We have to do something," said Ruby.

"But he might cast another spell!" Kirsty said.

"Even so, we have to help him, don't we?" Amber said firmly. All the other Rainbow Fairies agreed.

Kirsty felt so proud of them. The fairies were being very kind and brave.

"I know what to do!" Sky flew over the giant bubble. She looked nervous, being so close to Jack Frost, and she whispered her spell so quietly that Rachel and Kirsty couldn't hear the words.

A jet of blue fairy dust streamed out of Sky's wand and into the bubble. The dust swirled in a spiral, bigger and bigger, until it filled the whole bubble.

Rachel and Kirsty flew over and peered in.

The fairy dust had turned into huge crystal snowflakes. The water on Jack Frost's face froze into tiny drops of ice. He had stopped melting! The wind spun the snow

faster, whirling around Jack Frost in circles.

"Look! He's getting smaller and smaller!" Kirsty gasped.

She was right. First, Jack Frost was smaller than a goblin. Then, he was smaller than a squirrel, then, even smaller than Queenie the bee. Everyone looked from the bubble to Sky and back again. What was going to happen next?

With a loud *POP*, the bubble burst. The wind stopped and the snow vanished.

At first, Kirsty thought Jack Frost had completely disappeared. Then she noticed a very small glass globe lying on the grass. Inside

the globe, a tiny figure leaped around angrily.

"It's a snow globe!" Kirsty said in amazement. "And Jack Frost is trapped inside!"

Time for a Rainbow

"Hooray for Sky!" cried Rachel. "Now, Jack Frost can't hurt any of us, and we can take him safely back to Fairyland." Rachel flew over and picked up the snow globe. It felt smooth and cold, and it shook when Jack Frost jumped around inside.

Bertram hopped toward Rachel. "I'll take care of that, Miss Rachel," he said.

Rachel was glad to hand over the snow globe. She didn't like being so close to Jack Frost!

"Into the pot, everybody!" shouted Inky. "It's time to go back to Fairyland!"

"Yippee!" yelled Amber, doing a backflip in midair.

Heather waved her wand and the pot rolled upright, onto its four short legs. Rachel, Kirsty, and all of the fairies flew inside. Bertram the frog climbed in after them. It was a little cramped, but Rachel and Kirsty were too excited to care.

"Ready?" Ruby asked.

Her sisters nodded, looking very serious. The seven Rainbow Fairies raised their wands. There was a flash above them, like rainbow-colored fireworks. A fountain of sparks filled the pot with beautiful bold colors: red, orange, yellow, green, blue, indigo, and violet.

And then the brightest rainbow Rachel
and Kirsty had ever seen soared upward
into the clear blue sky.

With a *whoosh*, Bertram and the fairies
shot out of the pot, carried on the
rainbow like a giant wave. Rachel and
Kirsty felt themselves zooming up the
rainbow, too. Flowers, stars, leaves, tiny
butterflies, ink drops, and bubbles made of
fairy dust fizzed and popped around them.

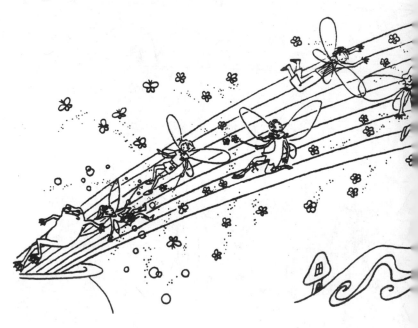

"This is amazing!" Kirsty shouted.
Far below, she could see hills dotted
with toadstool houses. It was Fairyland!
There was the winding river and the
royal palace with its four pointed towers.

All of a sudden, the rainbow vanished in a fizz of fairy dust. Kirsty and Rachel flapped their wings and drifted gently to the ground. Rachel looked around, expecting to see all the colors coming back to Fairyland.

But the hills and the toadstool houses were still gray!

"Why hasn't the color returned?" Rachel gasped.

Kirsty shrugged, too worried to speak.

One by one, the
Rainbow Fairies
landed softly
next to the
girls. And
Kirsty saw that
where each fairy
had landed on the
gray grass, a patch
of the greenest green
was spreading outward.

"Rachel, look!" Kirsty shouted.
"The grass is turning green!"

"Oh, yes!" Rachel said. Her eyes shone.

The fairy sisters stood in a circle and
raised their wands. A fountain of
rainbow-colored sparks shot up into the
fluffy, white clouds. There was a flash of
golden lightning, and it began to rain.

195

Rachel and Kirsty watched in delight
as tiny glittering raindrops, in every color
of the rainbow, pattered gently down
around them. And where they fell, the
color returned, flowing like shining paint
across everything in Fairyland.

The toadstool houses
gleamed red and
white. Brightly
colored flowers
dotted the green
hills with orange,
yellow, and purple.

The river was a bright, clear blue.

On the highest hill, the fairy palace
shone pink. Music came out as the front
doors of the palace slowly opened.

Ruby flew down to Rachel and Kirsty.
"Hurry!" she said. "The king and queen
are waiting for us."

Rachel and Kirsty flew toward the
palace with the seven fairies. Below
them, Bertram hurried along with
enormous leaps.

The Rainbow Fairies beamed as elves, pixies, and other fairies rushed out of the palace and danced around. "Hooray! Hooray for the Rainbow Fairies!" they cheered. "Hooray for Rachel and Kirsty!"

Queen Titania and King Oberon came out of the palace after them. The queen wore a silver dress and a sparkling diamond tiara. The king's coat and crown were made of gold.

"Welcome back, dear Rainbow Fairies. We have missed you," said Titania, holding out her arms. "Thank you a thousand times, Rachel and Kirsty!"

Bertram gave a deep bow. "This is for you, Your Majesty," he said, giving the snow globe to Oberon.

"Thank you, Bertram," said Oberon. He held the snow globe in both hands and looked into it. "Now, Jack Frost," he said sternly. "If I let you out, will you promise to stay in your icy castle and not harm the Rainbow Fairies again?"

"Remember that winter still belongs to you," Titania reminded him.

Inside the snow globe, Jack Frost stroked his sharp chin. "Very well," he said. "But on one condition."

"And what is that?" asked Oberon.

Kirsty looked at Rachel, suddenly feeling worried. What was he going to ask for?

"That I'm invited to the next Midsummer Ball," said Jack Frost.

Titania smiled. "You will be very welcome," she said kindly.

Oberon tapped the snow globe and it cracked in half. Jack Frost sprang out and shot up to his full, skinny height. Snow

glittered on his
white hair. He
snapped his fingers
and a sleigh made of
ice appeared next to
him. Hopping onto it,
he zoomed up into the sky.

All the fairies waved.

"Good-bye. We'll see you next year
at the Midsummer Ball!" Sky called
after him.

Jack Frost looked over his shoulder. A
smile flickered across his sharp face. Then,
he was gone.

Very Special Gifts

The Fairy King and Queen smiled
warmly at Rachel and Kirsty.

"Thank you, dear friends," said
Oberon. "Without you, Jack Frost's spell
never would have been broken."

"You will always be welcome in
Fairyland," Titania told them. "And

wherever you go, watch for magic. It will always find you."

The Rainbow Fairies fluttered over to say good-bye to the girls. Rachel and Kirsty hugged each one of them. They couldn't help feeling a little bit sad. They were going to miss their new friends very much.

Bertram hopped over and shook their hands. "Good-bye, Miss Rachel and Miss Kirsty. It was a pleasure to meet you," he said.

"Now, here's a special rainbow to take you home!" said Heather.

The fairy sisters raised their wands one more time. An enormous rainbow whooshed upward, stretching all the way back to Rainspell Island.

"Here we go!" Rachel shouted with joy as she felt herself being swept up by the glowing colors.

"I love riding on rainbows!" cried Kirsty.

Soon, Rainspell Island appeared below them. The girls landed with a soft thud in the backyard of Mermaid Cottage.

Follow a fairy to the end of the rainbow!

"Oh, we're back to our normal size," Rachel said, standing up.

"And we're just in time to catch the ferry!" Kirsty added as they ran around to the front yard.

"It's sad that our fairy adventures are over, isn't it?" Rachel said sadly.

Kirsty nodded. "But remember what Titania said about magic finding us from now on!"

"There you are," said Rachel's mom as the girls ran into the front yard. "Did you see that beautiful rainbow? And it wasn't even raining. Rainspell Island is a really special place!"

Kirsty and Rachel shared a secret smile.

"The car's packed. Check your bedroom to see if you've left anything behind," said Kirsty's mom.

Kirsty dashed into Dolphin Cottage and went upstairs.

"I'll check mine, too!" Rachel hurried into Mermaid Cottage and ran upstairs to her little attic

 207

room for the last time. She stopped in her bedroom doorway. "Oh!" She gasped.

In the middle of the bed, something shone and glittered like a huge diamond.

Rachel walked closer. It was a snow globe, full of fluttering fairy-dust shapes in all the colors of the rainbow.

"It's the most beautiful thing I've ever seen," Rachel said. She scooped up the glass globe and dashed next door. Kirsty was running down the stairs. She held an identical snow globe in her hands. "I'm going to keep this forever!" she said.

The two friends smiled at each other. "Every time I shake my snow globe, or see a rainbow, it will make me think of you, and Fairyland, and all the Rainbow Fairies," said Rachel as they left the cottage.

"Me, too!" replied Kirsty. "We'll *never* forget our secret fairy friends."

"No, we won't," said Rachel. "*Never.*"

Hannah the Happily Ever After Fairy

Hannah
the Happily
Ever After
Fairy

The Counter

Welcome to Tippington Bookstore

Magic Quill

Jack Frost's Desk

Guide to Goblins
A WINTER'S TALE @
What they Never Told You
Holly the Christmas Fairy
Amber the Orange Fairy
A Sudden Chill
Finding Fairies ☆
Fairies: Do they really exist?

Kylie the Carnival Fairy
Stella the Star Fairy

Fairy tale Shelf

Goldilocks @
Hansel and Gretel
The Princess and the Pea
The Little Matchstick Girl
The Little Mermaid
Jack and the Beanstalk
SNOW WHITE
The Snow Queen
Sleeping Beauty
Rapunzel
The Three Little Pigs
Beauty and the Beast
Cinderella
Puff, The Magic Dragon
Ali Baba
Red Riding Hood
The Princess & the Frog

Children's Corner

For Hannah Powell,
with lots of love and
happily ever afters.

Special thanks to
Narinder Dhami

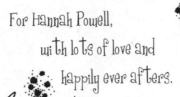

Unhappy Endings

"Once upon a time," Kirsty Tate began, "there was a girl named Cinderella. . . ."

Kirsty's best friend, Rachel Walker, smiled as she looked out at the children in the audience. They were listening quietly to Kirsty, their eyes wide. Rachel and Kirsty had offered to read a story in

the children's corner at Tippington
Bookstore. Now they were sitting with
the children in the cozy reading area,
surrounded by shelves of books.

Kirsty went on with the story. " 'Oh!'
Cinderella sighed. 'I'd love to go to the

ball!' But her stepsisters glared at her and said . . ." Kirsty glanced at Rachel, who was doing the voices of the wicked stepsisters.

" 'You won't be going to the ball!' " Rachel said in a snooty voice, making the children giggle. " 'You're just a servant dressed in rags!' "

"Nice job!" Kirsty whispered to Rachel, turning the page.

"And Cinderella's evil stepsisters made sure that Cinderella did not go to the ball," Kirsty read. "Instead, she

stayed at home and cleaned the house. Her stepsisters came home and told Cinderella all about the handsome prince . . ."

The children gasped in horror. Kirsty's voice trailed off as she realized what she'd just read. She had never read a version of *Cinderella* where she didn't go to the ball! Flustered, Kirsty glanced at Rachel. Her friend looked just as confused.

"Kirsty," a little girl called out anxiously, "how will Cinderella live happily ever after if she doesn't go to the ball?"

"Check the rest of the story, Kirsty," Rachel whispered.

Kirsty flipped ahead a few pages.

Cinderella was still sweeping and dusting, and her stepsisters were still being mean to her. Even on the very last page, Cinderella was dressed in rags, and her stepsisters were complaining that she hadn't washed their clothes properly!

"It's a different story," Kirsty whispered to Rachel. "There's no happy ending!"

Some of the children were looking very worried.

"Let's make the story up," Rachel suggested quietly. "After all, we know what *should* happen!"

"Good idea," Kirsty agreed. She raised
her voice. "So, on the night of the ball,
Cinderella was sitting sadly by the fire.
Suddenly, out of nowhere, there was a
dazzling puff of glittering smoke!"

"It's Cinderella's Fairy Godmother!"
the children shouted happily.

To Rachel and
Kirsty's relief, the
children didn't realize
that the girls were
making the story up as
they went along. They
kept going, and their
audience listened,
wide-eyed, until the
very end.

". . . and Cinderella
and the prince lived happily ever after."
Kirsty finished. The children clapped.

"This book is really strange, Rachel,"
Kirsty said, as the kids began trickling
back to their parents.

"I know," Rachel agreed, taking the
book and flipping through the pages.

"Do you think
Charlie knows?"
The girls glanced
over at Charlie, the
bookstore owner.
He was busy at the
computer near
the counter, but
he looked up and
waved at them.

"Good work, girls!" he called. "I'll
be closing up soon, but you can wait
here until Rachel's mom comes to pick
you up."

"Look, Rachel," Kirsty said, pointing at
one of the bookshelves. "There are lots of
fairy tales here. Let's check the endings."

Rachel picked up a different copy of
Cinderella and checked the last page.

Again, the story
ended with
Cinderella in rags.

Meanwhile, Kirsty
opened *Rapunzel*.
"Rachel!" She
gasped. "Rapunzel's
still stuck in the
tower at the end of
this story!"

Now Rachel was flipping through *Snow White*. She showed Kirsty the last page. ". . . and Snow White was trapped in her glass case forever!" Rachel read aloud.

"All the stories have unhappy endings!" Kirsty exclaimed, opening *The Little Mermaid*. "Oh, no they don't!" she corrected herself, handing the book to Rachel. "Look, the Little Mermaid marries her prince!"

But as the girls peered at the book, the words seemed to blur and swim. The last sentence was changing before their very eyes!

Now it said, "The Little Mermaid didn't marry the prince, and she didn't live happily ever after."

"This is so weird!" Kirsty whispered, reaching for a *Sleeping Beauty* pop-up book. "It seems like magic!"

"But it can't be fairy magic," Rachel added. "Not with sad endings!"

The girls knew all about fairy magic, because they were friends with the fairies! Rachel and Kirsty had helped them many times before when cold, icy Jack Frost and his goblins caused trouble.

Kirsty opened *Sleeping Beauty*, and a
beautiful silver and blue cardboard
castle popped up. The next moment,
a glittering shower of silver fairy dust
burst from the book and swirled
around the girls. As the sparkles drifted
through the air, Rachel and Kirsty
spotted a tiny fairy perched on the castle
balcony!

"Hello, girls!" the fairy called eagerly,
waving at them.

A Sneaky Thief

The fairy flew up to join Rachel and Kirsty, her blue dress shimmering. She wore a daisy necklace and belt, and dainty blue ballet shoes.

"I'm Hannah the Happily Ever After Fairy," she said, landing on Rachel's shoulder. "And I really need your help!"

"Of course!" Kirsty said quickly. "What happened?"

"Does it have something to do with the unhappy endings?" Rachel asked.

Hannah nodded, her blond curls bobbing. "I'm in charge of the magic Quill in Fairyland," she explained. "But yesterday, Jack Frost snuck into the palace and stole it!"

"What does the Quill do?" Kirsty asked anxiously.

"It has the power to write fairy tales," said Hannah. "But that's not all — the magic Quill can also change them!"

"Oh!" Rachel gasped. "So that's what Jack Frost is doing with the Quill. He's rewriting the endings of all the fairy tales to make them unhappy!"

"Yes," Hannah replied, her wings drooping. She looked very sad. "When Jack Frost writes an unhappy ending for a story with the magic Quill, every copy of that story in every

bookstore, library, school, or home around the world changes! All he has to do is write the title of the story he wants to change at the top of the page."

The girls looked at each other in horror.

"That's terrible!" Kirsty cried. "We have to stop him!"

"Yes, we must get the magic Quill back!" Rachel agreed.

Hannah smiled. "I knew you'd want to help, girls!" she said gratefully. "But it's going to be tricky. We don't know where Jack Frost is. All we know is that he escaped into the human world with the Quill!"

Just then, the store bell jingled as a customer came in.

"Charlie's about to close up, so that's probably my mom," Rachel said.

Hannah and the girls poked their heads around the bookshelves to see if Mrs. Walker had arrived.

But instead of Rachel's mom, Jack Frost himself was standing inside the door, staring around the bookstore with an icy gaze!

A Cool Customer

Rachel and Kirsty could hardly believe their eyes. Jack Frost had used his magic to make himself much taller — as tall as the highest tower of the Fairyland Palace! Icicles hung from his beard. He looked more frightening than ever! He carried a large bag,

and six ugly goblins stood right
behind him.

Hannah put her wand to her lips.
"Don't make a sound, girls," she
whispered. "The Quill must be in that
bag!"

Rachel and Kirsty watched as Jack
Frost stomped over to the counter.

"I'm sorry, we're just about to close —"
Charlie began, but then he glanced up
and saw his new customer. His mouth
fell wide open.

Jack Frost raised his
wand. "With this magic
spell of mine, I freeze
you here in space
and time," he
chanted. "When
I leave, you will
be free, but
you will not
remember me!"

Rachel and
Kirsty watched
with wide eyes as
Charlie froze
where he stood,

the look of shock
still on his face.
Ice frosted his hair
and clothes, and
long, glittering
icicles hung
from his nose
and ears.

"What's Jack
Frost doing here?" whispered Kirsty.
Hannah and Rachel shrugged.

Jack Frost turned to his goblins. "I've
changed all the fairy tales I can think
of," he told them. "But there must
be more."

He pointed at the bookshelves with his
wand. "Find any stories that still have
happy endings and bring them to me!"

Rachel and Kirsty looked at each other
in panic. They were standing right in the
middle of the fairy tale section!

"This way, girls!" Hannah whispered,
flying into the next aisle.

Rachel and Kirsty crept after her,
away from the fairy tales. Once they

were out of sight, the girls peeked around the bookshelves to watch Jack Frost and his goblins.

The goblins were fighting with each other, pushing and shoving and trying to be the first to find each of the fairy tales.

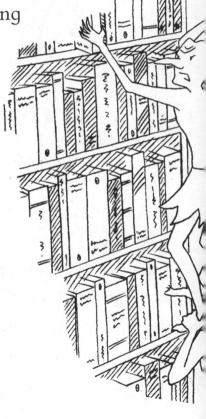

"Get out of my way!" cried one.

"I want to find a fairy tale for Jack Frost!" yelled another.

"They're making a huge mess," Rachel whispered.

The goblins pulled handfuls of
books off the shelves and tossed
them aside. Some of the
goblins stood on
each other's
shoulders to reach
the higher
shelves, then
threw the books
to the floor.
"Look at Jack
Frost," Hannah
whispered.
Jack Frost had
made his way to the
counter and was now
taking two piles of paper
out of his bag. The girls

could see that the pages in one pile had writing on them, but the pages in the other were blank. Once the papers were arranged on the counter, Jack Frost opened his bag again. He carefully pulled out a long feather that glittered with all the colors of the rainbow.

"The magic Quill!" Hannah breathed.

The Quill shimmered as Jack Frost picked up a blank piece of paper.

"There won't be a single *happily ever after* in any of the fairy tales by the time I'm finished!" he said, grinning cruelly as he began to write. Wherever the Quill touched the paper, magical, multicolored sparkles shot in all directions.

"We have to get that Quill back!" whispered Rachel.

"But how?" asked Kirsty with a frown.

Suddenly, a shout from one of the goblins startled the girls.

"This book still has a happy ending!" the goblin cried, waving a copy of *Hansel and Gretel*. "I'll take it to Jack Frost!"

"No, I saw it first!" another goblin yelled, trying to grab the book. "Give it to me!"

The goblin holding the book dashed off toward Jack Frost.

The other goblin immediately began to

run, too, shrieking with rage. He threw himself at the first goblin and grabbed his legs, sending him crashing into Jack Frost's counter. Both piles of paper went flying.

"You fools!" Jack Frost roared.

One of the pages landed near Rachel, and she picked it up. "Cinderella doesn't go to the ball, she doesn't marry the prince, and she lives horribly  ever after!" it said in rainbow-colored ink.

"These pages must be all the unhappy endings Jack Frost has written with the Quill," Hannah whispered.

"How can I get any work done with you around?" Jack Frost yelled at the bumbling goblins. He grabbed his wand. "So you won't be able to bother me at all, I hereby make you quiet and small!" he shouted.

An icy cloud of fairy dust streamed out of Jack Frost's wand and filled the store. It

swirled around the goblins, who instantly shrank down to fairy-size. Hannah quickly zoomed up to the ceiling, away from the magic dust, but Rachel and Kirsty were caught in Jack Frost's spell.

"Kirsty!" Rachel gasped, as the magic dust cleared. "We shrank, too!"

Kirsty looked at Rachel. "We're the same size as Hannah now, just like when the fairies make us small," she added, as Hannah flew back to join them. "But, look," she went on, pointing to her friend's shoulders. "This time we don't have any wings!"

Girls Go Into Action

"What did you say?" Rachel asked with a frown. Kirsty's voice was so tiny and quiet, she could hardly hear her! It was only when she glanced over her own shoulder that she realized what Kirsty meant.

The girls stared at each other in shock. They had become fairy-sized

many times before — but they'd always had wings!

On the other side of the bookshelves, which towered above the girls like skyscrapers, Jack Frost was picking up his papers and grumbling at the goblins.

"He left the Quill on the counter," Rachel pointed out. "Now's our chance!"

"Can you make us human-sized again?" Kirsty asked Hannah eagerly.

Hannah shook her head. "I can't undo Jack Frost's spell," she replied sadly.

"That means that even if we get onto the counter, we can't pick up the Quill," Kirsty said glumly. "It's too big."

"Well, I can't make you big . . . but I *can* make the Quill small!" Hannah exclaimed.

"Great idea!" Kirsty sighed with relief. "But how will we get onto the counter? It's too high for us to reach!"

"Look," Rachel said, pointing to a stack of books on the floor. "Hannah, could you use your magic to make those books into a staircase?"

Hannah nodded. The girls watched as magic sparks flew from her wand. The

books immediately
organized themselves
into a staircase!
Rachel and Kirsty
ran over and began
to climb.

"Almost there,
girls!" Hannah
called, fluttering
above them.
"Keep going!"

As she climbed higher,
Rachel glanced over
her shoulder. Her
heart sank. The goblins
were jumping up and
down and pointing —
the girls had been
spotted!

"Kirsty!" Rachel gasped. "The goblins have seen us. They're trying to warn Jack Frost!"

Kirsty glanced at Jack Frost. "He hasn't noticed yet," she said. "He can't hear the goblins now that they're so small, but we'd better hurry!"

Rachel and Kirsty stepped off the last book and onto the counter. They'd made it — and they could see the magic Quill shimmering and sparkling not far away! But the goblins had given up trying to warn Jack Frost. Now they were climbing up the book staircase after the girls.

"They're coming!" Kirsty cried. "Quick, Hannah, make the Quill smaller!"

Hannah sent a swirl of fairy dust toward the Quill, shrinking it to the size of a

teaspoon. "The goblins are blocking your way down, girls!" she warned. "How are you going to get away?"

Rachel looked around desperately for an escape route, but she couldn't see a way out. There was nothing on the counter except the Quill and some blank pieces of paper, and the counter was far too high for them to jump off of.

Suddenly, as she stared at the magic Quill, Rachel had an idea. She knew the Quill had the power to change stories, so what if she turned everything that was happening right now into a story? A story called: *Hannah the*

Happily Ever After Fairy! If Rachel wrote
the ending to the story now, maybe the
Quill's magic would make it happen!

Quickly, Rachel grabbed the sparkling
Quill.

"What are you doing?" asked Kirsty.

But Rachel didn't have time to reply.
On top of one of the blank pages she
wrote the title of her story: *Hannah the*

Happily Ever After Fairy. Rainbow-colored sparkles fizzed from the Quill as she wrote, and the glitter of magic caught Jack Frost's eye.

"Who's using my Quill?" he shouted from the back of the store.

"Hurry, Rachel!" Kirsty called. "The goblins have reached the top of the staircase, and Jack Frost spotted us! He's raising his wand to cast a spell!"

The Wind of Change

"I'm almost done!" Rachel cried.

Kirsty peered over Rachel's shoulder to see what she had written. Under the title, it said, "In the end, a fierce wind blew Jack Frost and all of his goblins far, far away!"

The moment Rachel finished writing "away," Kirsty felt a strong wind begin

to pick up. Just as the goblins stepped onto the countertop, the wind whisked them off their feet and swept them up into the air. The goblins shouted in confusion.

Jack Frost rushed toward the counter, pointing his wand at the girls. But in a flash, the wind scooped him up, too.

"Put me down!" Jack Frost cried as he was carried along helplessly on the strong breeze. "I'm Jack Frost! Put me down, I say!"

As Hannah and the girls watched, the store door flew open. The wind blew Jack Frost and all his goblins outside. Then it carried them high up into the evening sky, struggling and shouting all the way.

"Hooray, Rachel!"
Hannah laughed,
clapping her hands.

But Rachel was still
writing. Curious, Kirsty
and Hannah looked to
see what else she had
added.

"The fairy tales got their happy endings
back, and Charlie, Kirsty, Hannah, and
Rachel lived happily ever after!"

Immediately, Rachel and Kirsty shot back up to their normal size and had to scramble down off the counter. To their delight, they saw that Charlie wasn't frozen anymore, either. He was typing away at the computer, just as he had been doing when Jack Frost arrived. He gave the girls a cheerful smile, as Hannah ducked out of sight behind Kirsty.

"Your mom will probably be here soon, Rachel," he said, and disappeared into the stockroom.

"What a relief!" Hannah smiled. "Jack Frost's spell means that Charlie doesn't remember anything. Now let's clean up before he gets back!"

She waved her wand. The girls watched as books magically lifted themselves off the floor and jumped back onto the shelves in a swirl of glittering fairy magic.

"If you ever need help with your own stories," Hannah said with a smile, "just come to Fairyland and find me!"

"Thank you," Rachel said, smiling.

"Don't forget the Quill," Kirsty added picking up the tiny, feathery pen and handing it carefully to Hannah.

"Everyone in Fairyland will be very grateful," said Hannah, her eyes shining. "And so will everyone who reads fairy tales! Good-bye, girls. Thank you!"

Hannah and the Quill
disappeared in a
cloud of magical
sparkles.

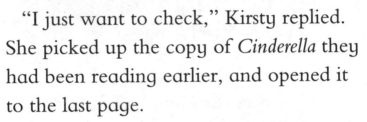

"What are you
doing?" Rachel
asked, as Kirsty
hurried over to the
children's corner.

"I just want to check," Kirsty replied.
She picked up the copy of *Cinderella* they
had been reading earlier, and opened it
to the last page.

Then Rachel and Kirsty beamed at
each other. The fairy tale ended exactly
as it should: "Cinderella married her
prince, and they lived happily ever after!"

Read all the books in the

series!

Here's a special peek at
Weather Fairies #1:

Crystal the
Snow Fairy!

A Magical Surprise

"Isn't it a beautiful day, Mom?" Kirsty
Tate asked happily. She gazed out of the
car window at the blue sky and sunshine.
"Do you think it will stay like this for all
of summer vacation?"

Mrs. Tate laughed. "Well, let's hope so,"
she said. "But remember what the weather

was like on Rainspell Island? It was always changing!"

Kirsty smiled to herself. She and her parents had been to Rainspell Island for vacation during the last school break. Kirsty had made a new friend there, Rachel Walker, and the two girls now shared a very special secret. They were friends with the fairies!

"Could Rachel come and stay with us for a little while, Mom? Please?" Kirsty asked, as they pulled up outside their house.

"That's a really good idea," Mrs. Tate agreed. "Now, let's take this stuff inside."

"OK," said Kirsty, climbing out of the car. "Where's Dad?"

Just then, a voice called out from the distance. "Hello, I'm up here!"

Kirsty glanced up, shading her eyes against the sun. To the left of the house was an old wooden barn. Mr. Tate was standing at the top of a ladder next to the barn, holding a hammer.

"I'm just repairing the barn roof," he explained. "It's been leaking."

Suddenly, Kirsty jumped. Something cold and wet had landed on her nose! "Oh no!" she exclaimed. "I think it's raining." Then she stared at the white flakes that had landed on her pink shirt. "It's not rain," she gasped. "It's *snow*!"

"Snow?" Mrs. Tate looked shocked. "In summer? It can't be!"

There's magic in every book!

The Rainbow Fairies
Books #1-7

The Weather Fairies
Books #1-7

The Jewel Fairies
Books #1-7

The Pet Fairies
Books #1-7

The Fun Day Fairies
Books #1-7

SCHOLASTIC

www.scholastic.com
www.rainbowmagiconline.com

HiT entertainment